P Is For Passover

A Holiday Alphabet Book

By Tanya Lee Stone
Illustrated by Margeaux Lucas

PSS!
PRICE STERN SLOAN

A is for afikomen

The search will be fun
The broken matzah is hidden
And our story's begun!

B is for burning bush

Flames Moses saw
God sent him a message
He listened in awe!

C is for charoset

Nuts, apples, and wine
We eat it at Seder
Add cinnamon to mine!

D is for Dayenu

The "Thank You" we sing
For all God has brought us
For freedom, each spring!

E is for Elijah

Front door opens wide!
We fill up his wine cup,
Will he come inside?

Da-da-ye-nu
Da-da-ye-nu
Da-da-ye-nu

HAGGADAH

F is for feast

Seder meal we share
To honor our freedom
I relax in my chair!

G is for gefilte fish

Gram makes it from scratch
Put horseradish on it,
I'll eat the whole batch!

H is for Haggadah

Let's follow along
Read the Passover story
And sing every song!

HAGGADAH

הגדה

I is for infant

Adrift in the water
Found in a basket
By pharaoh's young daughter.

J is for journey

We relive it each year,
A trip 'cross the desert
To a land free from fear.

K is for Knaidels
So fluffy and hot
Matzah balls in my soup
Sure hit the spot!

L is for L'chaim
"To life!" we all cheer
Aunts, uncles, and cousins
All join us each year!

M is for matzah

Flat bread made of wheat
Quickly baked before fleeing
It's crispy to eat!

N is for Nisan

Full moon rises bright
When Passover starts
On this month's 15th night.

O is for *One Little Goat*

A song that I love
The goat gets in trouble,
And is saved from above.

P is for Passover
Or Pesach, some say,
We celebrate freedom
On this holiday!

Q is four questions
My brother recites
"Why is this night different
From all other nights?"

R is for Red Sea
That parted so wide
How everyone danced
When they reached the far side!

S is for Seder Plate
Filled with five things
Taste the maror
And the bitterness it brings!

maror (bitter herbs)

Karpas (fresh greens)

charoset

zeroa (shank bone)

baytzah (roasted egg)

T is for ten plagues,
Gave Pharaoh a fright,
Hail, grasshoppers, frogs
And day turned to night!

U is for unleavened bread

And also sweet cakes
My favorite's the brownies
That Dad always makes!

V is for vegetables

To remember slave-years,
They're dipped in salt water,
Which reminds us of tears.

W is for wine

That Aunt Liz helps me pour
I fill each glass once
And again three times more!

X is in eXodus

That Moses once led
Away from the pharaoh
The Hebrews all fled!

Mah nishtanah . . .

Y is for the youngest
Who plays a big part
A small person asking
Four questions, so smart!

HAGGADAH

Zzzzzz is the sleepy sound
Tired kids make
The Seder was fun
But we can't stay awake!